Contents

CHAPTER 1
Oh, What a Kite! 1

CHAPTER 2
Let's Fly! 4

CHAPTER 3
If at First You Don't Succeed ... 11

CHAPTER 4
On the Loose 18

CHAPTER 5
Major Trouble 23

EXTRA STUFF

• Kite Lingo 33

• Kite Must-dos 34

• Kite Instant Info 36

• Think Tank 38

• Hi Guys! (Author Letter) 40

• When We Were Kids 42

• What a Laugh! 43

Nick   *Matt*

CHAPTER 1

Oh, What a Kite!

Nick and Matt are best friends. After working for three weeks, they have saved enough money to buy a kite. Today they have taken it to the local park to try it out.

Matt   "This is so cool! Having our own kite."

Nick "Yes, now we're going to know what it feels like to be a bird."

Matt "I'd love to be a bird."

Nick "What sort of bird would you want to be?"

Matt "Well, if I was a bird I'd want to be an eagle. Eagles rule the sky."

Nick "If I was a bird, I'd be a pigeon."

Matt "What's so great about pigeons?"

Nick "Pigeons never get lost. They always know how to find their way home."

Matt "That would be good around dinner time!"

Nick "So, now that we've got the kite ready to go, what do we do?"

Matt "We launch it into the sky."

Nick "It's a kite, not a rocket ship."

CHAPTER 2

Let's Fly!

Nick and Matt attach the string to the kite.

Nick "So, all you have to do now is run as fast as you can while you hold on to the string."

Matt "How come I have to do all the running?"

Nick "Well, someone has to hold on to the kite and launch it."

Matt "OK, I suppose I can run a lot faster than you."

Nick "What? There's no way you can run faster than me."

Matt "So why don't you run with the string then?"

Nick "Time for a decider!"

Matt "Paper, scissors, stone!"

Nick "Ready ... one, two, three!"

Matt "Stone beats scissors. I win!"

Nick "You win. You get to run as fast as you can pulling a kite—yes, you really win."

Matt "Well, at least I get to fly the kite for the first time."

Matt holds on to the string while Nick holds the kite.

Matt "When I shout 'Now!' you let go of the kite."

Nick "Make sure that you run really fast."

Matt "I always run fast."

Matt yells "Now!" as loud as he can and then starts to run. The kite flies a couple of metres into the air and then falls to the ground.

Nick "You have to run faster than that!"

Matt "It's not my fault—there isn't any wind."

Nick (pointing at the top of the trees) "There's plenty of wind up there."

Matt "Yes, but that's up there, and we're down here."

Nick "Well, you just have to run faster."

Matt picks up the string.

Matt "OK, this time I'll really get it up there."

Matt starts to run again. This time the kite nearly gets to the top of the trees, but again it crashes to the ground. Nick also has a turn, but he can't get the kite into the air either.

CHAPTER 3

If at First You Don't Succeed ...

The boys discuss what they can
try next.

Matt "We have to think of a better
way to launch the kite."

11

Nick "We need more takeoff speed."

Matt (excitedly) "I know what to do! I know what to do!"

Nick "Well, stop jumping up and down and tell me."

Matt "We tie the kite to the back of the bike and ride really fast. That's sure to get the kite into the sky."

Nick "That's a cool idea!"

The boys attach the string to the back of Nick's bike. Matt stands back and holds the kite. Nick gets on the bike and is ready to pedal.

Matt "Ready, set, go!"

Nick starts pedalling. Matt lets the kite go and it heads for the sky.

13

Nick (laughing) "Hooray, our kite is in orbit!"

Nick unties the string from the bike and holds on to it.

Matt "This is great!"

Nick (pointing) "The kite looks so huge. I don't think there's a bird in the world that would be brave enough to come anywhere near our kite."

Matt "Can I have a turn?"

Nick passes the string to Matt.

Matt "Wow, it's hard to hold on to!"

Nick "If we tied it to one of the girls from down the street, she'd take off and be the first girl to land on the Moon."

Matt "Maybe we should go and find them and see if they do take off."

Nick "Yes, when people ask where they are we could tell them that they've gone to visit some of their relatives."

Matt "Do you want another go at holding the string?"

Nick "Yes!"

Matt starts to pass the string, but it slips from his hand. The kite breaks free and starts to fly across the sky.

CHAPTER 4

On the Loose

Nick and Matt are staring at their
kite as it floats away into the
distance. Both boys seem totally
shocked and don't seem to be able to
say anything until …

Matt "Why didn't you grab the string? You lost our kite."

Nick "Me? Lost the kite? *You* lost the kite. You didn't pass it to me properly."

Matt "Well, if we just stand here arguing, the kite is going to disappear forever."

Nick "We're going to have to move fast or we'll never catch it."

Matt "Quick! Get on your bike! We'll chase it."

The boys keep pedalling as fast as they can, watching the kite. Eventually it disappears over a hill. When the boys get to the top of the hill they're totally surprised to see their kite.

Matt (pointing) "There it is. Look! It's caught in that tree in the middle of the field."

Nick "Yes, all we have to do is climb the tree and we'll have our kite back."

Matt and Nick drop their bikes and
start to climb the fence. They don't
notice a large sign nailed to the fence
that says "Danger, do not enter".

CHAPTER 5

Major Trouble

Nick and Matt start to walk towards the tree in the middle of the field.

Matt "Next time we fly our kite we have to make sure that we tie the string around our hand."

Nick "You just have to make sure that you hold on to it!"

Matt "Yes right, it wasn't my fault."

All of a sudden Nick stops and grabs Matt's arm.

Nick "What's that noise?"

The boys turn around to see where the noise is coming from. Their mouths open wide in shock as they see the biggest bull they've ever seen running straight at them!

Matt and Nick "AAAARRRGHHHH!!!"

Matt "Let's get out of here."

Nick "Where are we going to go?"

Matt (pointing) "Let's climb up that tree."

The boys run to the tree and climb up. The bull, with steam blowing out of its nose, charges to the bottom of the tree and starts pawing the ground.

Nick (looking down) "Hope it can't climb trees."

Matt "If it can, we're dead."

The bull keeps pawing the ground and roaring.

Nick "I think that we're probably stuck here forever."

Matt "Yes, us, our kite and the bull."

Nick "So how do we get out of this mess?"

Just then, the boys hear the voices of what sounds like the girls from down the street. The girls laugh and start teasing the boys about not being able to read the sign.

Matt "Girls are so stupid."

Nick (shouting) "As if we would have
gone into the field if we'd read
the sign!"

Matt (to Nick) "How come *you* didn't
read the sign?"

Nick (to Matt) "How come *you* didn't read the sign?"

Matt "I was too busy looking at the kite."

Nick "Me too."

The girls ask the boys if they want some help.

Matt and Nick "Yes!"

The girls tell the boys that they'll go for help if the boys will let them have a turn flying the kite. The boys agree.

Nick "So, I wonder how long we're going to have to sit in this tree for?"

Nick and Matt look down at the bull.
The bull roars and paws at the ground.

Matt and Nick (yelling at the aliens
as they disappear) "If you hurry,
we'll *give* you the kite!!!!!"

Kite Lingo

Nick

Matt

flying line The flying line of the kite is the line that is used to control the kite.

frame The frame of a kite is the skeleton of the kite, which is covered with material.

kite A flying device that's often made of a wooden framework covered with paper, cloth or synthetic material.

large tree Where most kites seem to get tangled up.

tail A long strip of paper, plastic or ribbon that helps to balance the kite in flight! Not all kites need tails.

BOYS RULE!
Kite Must-dos

☞ Make sure that you hold on to the flying line really tightly.

☞ Don't get your flying line tangled.

☞ Don't fly your kite near trees. Kites seem to love trees.

☞ Make sure that you don't fly your kite near power lines. If you do, and the kite gets tangled, then it might be the last time you ever fly your kite.

☞ Never fly your kite in rain or lightning. Electricity in clouds is attracted to damp kite lines and crazy kite fliers.

☞ If it's a really windy day it might be a good idea to wear a rucksack with a brick in it so that you don't get pulled off the ground.

☞ Make sure that you wear trainers when you're flying your kite. You never know when your kite might break free and you have to chase it.

☞ Don't let someone who is really small hold on to your kite—they might take off and be lost forever.

☞ If your kite does break free and ends up in a field with a bull, then leave it there!

Kite Instant Info

No one knows where the first kites came from. Some people say that they began with the people of the South Sea Islands, who used kites to fish with. They used to attach bait and a net to the tail of the kite to catch the fish.

The largest kite ever flown is the Megabite, which is 64 metres long (including tails) and 22 metres wide, with a total flat area of 904 square metres.

There are kite clubs where people have competitions to see who can do the most tricks with their kites.

 Wind that is too strong or too light is difficult to fly a kite in. A flag or windsock is handy to help you see the wind.

 Remember, as the wind goes over and around trees and buildings, it gets bumpy and difficult to fly kites in. Watch out for kite-eating trees!

 Most kites are made of fibreglass or graphite.

BOYS RULE!
Think Tank

1 Should you fly your kite when there is a storm or should you stay inside and read a "Boys Rule!" book?

2 Is it dangerous to fly your kite near power lines?

3 If your kite gets stuck in the top of a tree, should you cut the tree down or hope that a strong wind might blow the kite down?

4 Can you have more than one flying line?

5 Is there more than one type of kite?

6 There is a bird called a kite. True or false?

7 Can kites fly if there is no wind?

8 What should you do if your kite lands in a field where there is a huge bull?

Answers

The following answers appear upside-down on the page:

1 You should stay inside during a storm or you might get struck by lightning.
2 Yes. You should keep well away from power lines.
3 If your kite gets stuck, you should hope that a strong wind blows it down.
4 Yes, and the more flying lines you have, the more tricks you can do.
5 Yes. Kites come in lots of different sizes and shapes.
6 True. There is a type of hawk called a kite.
7 No. You need a breeze to keep the kite in the sky.
8 Leave it there, go home and make another kite.

How did you score?

- If you got all 8 answers correct, then you're ready to build your own kite and go flying.

- If you got 6 answers correct, then you should buy a kite from a shop, but you could probably fly it pretty well.

- If you got fewer than 4 answers correct, then you probably should find something else to do. Flying kites just isn't your thing.

Felice →   ← Phil

Hi Guys!

We have heaps of fun reading and want you to, too. We both believe that being a good reader is really important and so cool.

Try out our suggestions to help you have fun as you read.

At school, why don't you use "Kite High" as a play and you and your friends can be the actors. Set the scene for your play. Bring some bits of wood, cloth and string to school to use as props. You might already have a kite at home that your parents would let you take to school. One of your friends can be the bull!

So ... have you decided who is going to be Nick and who is going to be Matt? Now, with your friends, read and act out our story in front of the class.

We have a lot of fun when we go to schools and read our stories. After we finish the children all clap really loudly. When you've finished your play your classmates will do the same. Just remember to look out the window—there might be a talent scout from a television channel watching you!

Reading at home is really important and a lot of fun as well.

Take our books home and get someone in your family to read them with you. Maybe they can take on a part in the story.

Remember, reading is fun.

So, as the frog in the local pond would say, Read-it!

And remember, Boys Rule!

When We Were Kids

Felice

Phil

Felice "Did you ever have a kite?"

Phil "I had the best kite ever."

Felice "Why was it so good?"

Phil "Well, I doubt a kite has ever been higher than my kite."

Felice "Oh yes?"

Phil "I'm serious. I'm sure a kite has never been higher."

Felice "Well, how high did your kite go?"

Phil "About 10,000 metres. I was in a plane coming home from holidays and had my new kite in my luggage!"

What a Laugh!

Q What do you say to a kite in flight?

A High kite!

BOYS RULE!

Gone Fishing

The Tree House

Golf Legends

Camping Out

Bike Daredevils

Water Rats

Skateboard Dudes

Tennis Ace

Basketball Buddies

Secret Agent Heroes

Wet World

Rock Star

Pirate Attack

Olympic Champions

Race Car Dreamers

Hit the Beach

Rotten School Day

Halloween Gotcha!

Battle of the Games

On the Farm